Samuel Nott

The Present Crisis

with a reply and appeal to European advisers, from the sixth edition of

Slavery and the remedy

Samuel Nott

The Present Crisis
with a reply and appeal to European advisers, from the sixth edition of Slavery and the remedy

ISBN/EAN: 9783337378363

Printed in Europe, USA, Canada, Australia, Japan

Cover: Foto ©Andreas Hilbeck / pixelio.de

More available books at **www.hansebooks.com**

The Present Crisis:

WITH A

REPLY AND APPEAL

TO

EUROPEAN ADVISERS,

FROM THE SIXTH EDITION OF

SLAVERY AND THE REMEDY.

BY

SAMUEL NOTT.

BOSTON:
CROCKER AND BREWSTER,
47 Washington Street.
1860.

THE PRESENT CRISIS.

AFTER the Sectional strife which has marked the closing and the opening year, it cannot be amiss to ask atttention to the REPLY AND APPEAL TO EUROPEAN ADVISERS, prefixed to the Sixth Edition of "Slavery and the Remedy." It has, at least, this advantage, that the subject is presented on the great principles required in a Plea before the Christian and philanthropic world, and that these are illustrated by instances, outside of the disturbed circle in which we move.

The principles thus illustrated, are,—The sovereignty of each separate State and the limited authority of the United States, removing the question of slavery in every form from the National Legislature;—The impossibility of any absolute and advantageous emancipation of the slaves, and the requirement, therefore, of all possible measures for their well-being;—and, finally, That Sectional impotence which limits the action of the North to whatever aids of wisdom and good-will.

These principles are more fully discussed in "Slavery and the Remedy," already widely circulated, but they cannot be obscure to those who shall read only the "Reply and Appeal." It is therefore sent abroad by itself, to the members of the National Legislature and to the principal officers of the several State Governments, in the hope of promoting the NEW ERA invoked at its close, and required no less by the interests of the African race, than by the fixed relations of North and South.

The necessity of some harmonizing principles in our great National family, was never more manifest and imperious than at the beginning of the year 1860. But no principles can effectually harmonize, save those which are merciful and just,—giving free scope to that " golden rule " which enriches those who obey it, even more than the objects of their self-proportioned good-will. The principles of advantageous Union must be at once National and beneficent; must unite the two great Sections with due regard to the welfare of all classes of the people.

If such harmonizing principles are discarded, nothing can be more fearful than the prospect before us. With Sections so substantially equal that no majorities or advantages can give to either an available supremacy, and so intimately united and dependant that separation is impossible, what else can ensue, but " the miserable strifes of those whom God has joined together in essential equality ?"—so much the more miserable because ruling and parting are alike impossible—the lasting curse of the European race, with only evil to the African, which is the subject of the strife.

The questions and the dangers wont to be uppermost in the public mind, seem to the writer to have no practical bearing—sink into utter insignificance, in the real relations of the two Sections to each other, and to those who are enslaved.

The question is not, for instance, whether free labor is more profitable than slave labor, now that we have four millions of slaves upon our hands, to be supported from the soil ;—and if supported *from* it, of necessity, to labor *on* it. There *is* the absolute necessity of food and raiment and shelter ; and the capital of the country cannot otherwise provide for it, than by regular, continuous and well-directed labor. The indispensable question *now*, is, How, justly and mercifully, to make the actual labor as available as possible, whether in restoring wasted soils, or in bringing virgin soils into cultivation ; so as to make the provision as permanent and increasing as the people to be provided for. If slave labor, from its inefficiency, or from its special burdens of infancy, sickness, and old age, be less profitable than free labor, neither Capital nor the State, is at liberty to make the change to the disadvantage of the present laborers,—with no adequate provision for them either at the North or the South.

Neither is it the question, Whether by means of free labor and its unlimited supply from the overflowing masses of Europe, the North will so surpass the South in wealth and numbers as to have the National Government in its hands, and be able to regulate and control the South according to *its* behest;—but, How shall the North and the South dwell together, as co-equal Sections, so as not to waste their energies and opportunity, either in equi-balanced impotence or equi-balanced contention. For, increasing wealth and numbers can never annihilate the fertile valleys which extend from the remotest North to the remotest South, nor the mineral stores which fill their mountain boundaries, nor the rivers which bear their products to the ocean, the common highway of both; nor the artificial connections which we have formed, according to the pre-arrangements of the Creator;—all making a mutual and co-equal inter-dependance, such as never existed in any Nation of the earth, or in any time before.

Wealth! numbers! the National Government in the hands of the North! The President and triumphant majorities against the South! What could these avail? Could they give efficient supremacy over a Section equi-balanced in fact, if not in form, by the fiat of the Omnipotent himself?—If there *were* all the advantages, vainly vaunted on one side and as vainly feared on the other, what could they avail in the equipoise, just as truly existing, as when the lighter weight has its equal power by means of the longer arm of the balance? Or, to take the illustration of the Body-politic, from the ancient fable;—God has so formed it, member by member and organ by organ, in mutual relations and dependance, by which each contributes to a healthful whole, so that it would be found as impossible for the North to rule the South, against its interests and its will, as for the hands or feet to debar the stomach from its equal place and influence in the whole system—from its full partnership in the healthful action and vital power of the rebellious and boastful limbs themselves.

And the danger is not, that the Union will be dissolved, and that we shall become two adjacent Nations, subject to alternate war and peace;—but, that an indissoluble Union will make more bitter a never-ceasing quarrel, without the intervals of peace, and the laws of Nations and of honor, which prevent or mitigate the horrors of inter-national war. Alas! for the North and the South, if they make of the twin brotherhood, which God has given them, "natural enemies," without the check of seas between them, of divided language, and the rules of war, as with the two kingdoms thus styled from the history of Centuries.

Neither is it the danger that the "Southern institution," will remain and extend itself into new Territories and States with all practicable ameliorations; but, that no Northern or Southern institution will arise instead, adequate to the wants of the African race, when directly or indirectly emancipated;—that "black codes," will prevail in the North and in the South, excluding them from place and opportunity, and rendering their freedom but a name. Alas! for them, if, by our "under-ground rail-roads," our border forays, and the "irrepressible conflict of free and slave labor," the increasing millions shall be freed;—when the South shall cast forth upon the resisting North, and the North shall drive back upon the resisting South, crowds upon crowds of Africans, freed, but not FREE;—with no place allowed for the sole of their foot, with no "free soil," from South to North and from ocean to ocean. Alas! for both races, European and African, if the harvest shall become ripe;—if Sectional distrust and hatred shall carry on a general and enduring war *against* the African freed, instead of the partial and fitful strife *for* the African enslaved, which may prove only the beginning of our troubles. If we will persist in sowing the wind, the time must come, when we shall "reap the whirlwind."

WAREHAM, MASS., MARCH 1, 1860.

ADVERTISEMENT

TO THE SIXTH EDITION.

THIS work was first published at the beginning of the year 1856. The Presidential Election at the close of that year and the Decision of the Supreme Court in the case of Dred Scott, gave occasion in the fourth and fifth editions for additional illustration of the principles which must govern the relations of the African and European races in the United States.

The several editions have been received with so much favor by some of the largest slave-holders, and by many eminent citizens and statesmen both North and South, as to encourage the belief that the work is not unfitted to its high purpose of engaging the Slave-holding States in their special duty to the African race, and of uniting the Free States in the only position for rendering effectual as well as acceptable aid.

With the deepest assurance that its principles and methods are such as Christian Philanthropy requires, we submit them as the true answer to the rebukes and demands of Foreign Societies and the Foreign Press, with such preliminary illustrations as European instances afford.

It will be found that we do not object to the interest taken in our affairs on the other side the Atlantic. We claim only, abroad as at home, that every proposal shall duly regard actual conditions and relations — shall seek a possible, substantial, and permanent good. He is our " neighbor," the wide world over, who even *advises* the " mercy " suited to our need.

REPLY AND APPEAL.

THE original design of "Slavery and the Remedy" was to fix the attention of the people of the United States upon the essential points of the question of slavery, now that the African race is to be regarded as settled in the land.

In executing this design we distinguished slavery, as a fact, from the proposal to enslave. Discarding the proposal, but requiring the fact to be treated as a fact, with due regard to actual conditions and relations, we turned the question from mere abolition and mere slavery to the well-being of the enslaved; and proposed a Remedial Code, as we believed, suited to the case and worthy to satisfy the conscience and philanthropy of the country by its beneficent character and tendency. At the same time we asserted the irresponsibility of the United States as a National Government, and the responsibility of each separate slaveholding State alone; and that the Free States, individually and socially, had no other obligation in the matter but to aid the work of well-being by all possible means of wisdom and good will.

In this edition we extend our design, and offer the

a *

principles and methods of this work to the consideration of those abroad, whose earnest remonstrances and appeals demand of the United States the abolition of slavery. The letters we receive, and the whole expression of the Foreign Press, seem to us utterly indiscriminate of facts and proposals — of the responsible and the irresponsible — the practicable and the impracticable — the advantageous and the disadvantageous — the right and the wrong.

We do not deny to European Philanthropists and Christians that right of interference which we have claimed for ourselves — the right of Christian goodwill, which is as wide as the world. "There is no evil on the face of the earth, which may not be rightly discussed, and for which just relief may not be attempted by any man on the face of the earth. Man to man, may speak for man, under no other restriction but to speak the words of truth, justice, and kindness, and no man or people has the right to gainsay." * We object only to the indiscriminate outcry, not to the benevolent intention. On the other hand, as it was our desire to engage in aid of the best measures of well-being our own Northern Philanthropy, so it is now, to engage that of Europe also to the same high purpose, both, as we believe, equally misdirected, to the injury of the very cause they profess to promote.

No doubt it is too much to assume that the Remedial Code proposed is absolutely perfect. Yet, with all readiness to question the details, we have the

* Page 47.

utmost confidence in the great principle on which it proceeds, *of meeting an existing fact as a fact, and not as a proposal,* and therefore of turning the question from abolition to well-being, from the irresponsible to the responsible; of breaking only the bad bonds and retaining the good, both of master and slave, until, the word slavery remaining or disappearing, the whole condition of Africa in America shall be such as is due to a Christian country and a Christian age. We do not propose to the responsible States to omit any duty to which a true Christian philanthropy calls — to cancel in regard to slavery one jot or tittle of the golden rule. Whatever ills attach to the African or the European race in point of fact, this work adopts them no more for the one than for the other; and requires equally for both all possible reliefs and benefits. It is not therefore to justify any wrong, to apologize for any removable evil, that this work is now offered to the consideration of our European advisers, but to engage their co-operation and influence in the work of good will to man required by the actual facts of African slavery in the United States. To this end we submit some introductory illustrations — suited, as we think, to correct their mistaken views.

1. One error of our foreign friends consists in addressing their Appeals to the citizens of the United States, as if in their National capacity, they were responsible for slavery in the several slave-holding States, in any other than the general sense, in which the Appellants themselves are responsible for the social conditions of the several European Nations, or

even for American slavery itself. We ask their careful attention to the argument,* showing who are, in the matter of slavery, ordained of God as the " Powers that be." Surely they must see that, by the ordinance of Heaven, the authority in all matters existing in 1776, and not transferred to the *United* States, *is* with each separate State; precisely as the authority of Great Britain, France, Austria, Prussia, or Russia, is over the social conditions of *each* of those nations, and not in any Congress of nations, whether temporary and special, or fixed and permanent like the American Union. No majorities in the august assemblies of such a Congress would have authority from HIM by whom " kings reign and princes decree justice," to abolish the serfdom of Russia, to restore the lost rights of the French Noblesse, to divide the domains of the Landholders of Great Britain, and to equalize the whole social condition of the high and the low in Austria and Prussia. These matters belong, by the ordinance of Heaven, to each several nation for itself; each has its own separate authority and responsibility. Any appeal in regard to them must be made to each by itself, and not to the whole as a Congress of Nations. In like manner the United States are not to be appealed to in regard to the social condition of the several States existing when their Union was formed. The general interests, which their common language and peculiar circumstances and an overruling Providence have enabled them to unite, giving them some advantage over adjacent European States

---

* Chapters VII. — XII.

do not destroy the limits by which God, for wise purposes, made them separate; give them no authority over the original and inherent right of each separate sovereignty.

Besides — if there were the authority of the whole over the parts in the matter in question — there is lacking the power by which alone authority can have vitality. If, as we have asserted and shown,* an overruling Providence has made an equilibrium between the slave-holding and the free States — if any supposable Northern majorities are counterbalanced by some compensatory powers of Southern minorities, then, any original authority would become nugatory by means of equibalanced forces, and all vital authority would cease. Equity itself can give no authority to equibalanced impotence; — can impose no duty.

Of this principle, take the most marked of European instances; Great Britain and France. — Is either responsible for the social condition of the other? Has either received from the Ruler of nations authority over the other; or, if the authority were claimed has either the power to overrule the other? In matters of essential equity has either the might, which alone could give the right, to overthrow the social conditions of the other? In such a warfare, can either acquire the responsibility of conquest; — the right and the duty of the stronger? Let centuries of war and blood answer the question which, in regard to its own relations, it behooves the New

* Chapter X.

World to answer by anticipation — before rival sections become "natural enemies," from generation to generation. Centuries of blood have given proof to all nations and all time, that God constituted Great Britain and France, two and not one, with no rightful authority and no overruling power in either. The Norman conquerors of England became successful only by the wisdom of forgetting France and becoming English. "The Kings of Great Britain, France, and Ireland," despite the claims and gifts and wars of generations, possessed but the empty title, could neither rule nor overrule the kingdom whose name they claimed. The strength which God gave them to rule their own fair domain, proved itself only impotence in the vain attempt to rule the neighboring kingdom, which God had made equal to themselves. Surely Great Britain is not to be appealed to, to abolish any social conditions of France, nor France, to abolish any social conditions of Great Britain, for God has given to neither nation, authority and power to rule and overrule the other — has not given the "might" which could make the "right," though the equity of the change were as clear as the noon-day.

With some differences indeed, but for reasons substantially similar, i. e., for lack of original authority and for equibalanced impotence, the Northern States are not to be appealed to in the matter of Southern slavery, neither in the National Congress, nor in any other way. Whatever may be the error of the South — God has given to the North neither authority nor power — has left them no other method but that of wise and friendly counsel. Impotence is not responsible for the acts of power. The palsied arm has no duties.

2. A second mistake of our Foreign Advisers is, the demand for the abolition of slavery on the ground of political consistency, in view of the Declaration of Independence and the Constitution of the United States. If we had National authority and power, does political consistency require it? In answer to this question, let us seek for European illustration.

Let then the Documents of English liberty be compared — the true sources and patterns of our own. Did they require, — did they furnish equal immunities for all classes of the people, homogeneous though they were, without regard to actual conditions, to the forms and arrangements which years and ages previous had introduced and established? Did Magna Charta, did the Bill of Rights, equalize all orders and ranks of men? Let these documents be considered.

Magna Charta, then, reclaimed the ancient rights of the Barons of England against the encroachments of the Crown; — no doubt enabling and requiring them to promote the well-being of their serfs, then the largest class, the great mass of the people; but neither enabling nor requiring them to abolish serfdom and make their serfs politically and personally free, to the injury of both. The *Bill of Rights* reclaimed the ancient rights of the Lords and Commons of England against new encroachments of the Crown, in like manner enabling and requiring all practicable advantages for all classes of the people, but neither enabling nor requiring equal suffrage to the entire mass without distinction ; — left unchanged the existing franchises and those relations of property and labor which doomed the mass to the actual condition of "the poor," without a voice in the government of their country. It was never claimed that Magna Charta and the Bill of Rights equalized all classes of society actually existing at their date. *These documents went as far as they went and no farther,* and left all matters unnamed, to the slow progress of just principles in promoting the well-being of all orders of the people. No doubt there has been wrong in not using the powers reclaimed for the well-being of the laboring and struggling masses, but it was never intended by these documents that all conditions of society should have *one* rule and *one* measure of civil liberty. In the language of Macaulay with regard to the Bill of Rights, "They made nothing law, which had not been law before. . . . Their object was to make the restoration of a tyrant impossible, and to place upon the throne sovereigns under whom law and liberty might be secure " * with all practicable advantages for all conditions of men.

In like manner, the 'Documents of the American Revolution — the Declaration of Independence and the Constitution of the United States, *went as far as they went and no farther, did what they did and no more ;* reclaimed English principles for English men, and not for the native Indians, or the Africans settled in the land, neither of whom had any such principles to reclaim, or were prepared to receive and enjoy the freedom of an English people; though the ruling quality assumed in those documents by the United "Englands" of America required from each all possible provision for every condition of people in any way under their government, whether to regulate their freedom or to ameliorate their slavery. These American documents "made nothing law which was not law before;" and the American Revolution stands precisely in the same relation to existing facts, as do the two great eras of British liberty — making no immediate changes in the relation of any inhabitants of the land, and yet containing the elements, and therefore the obligation, of progressive improvement for all. At the time of the Declaration of Independence, slavery, like serfdom in Great Britain eight hundred years ago, existed in every state but one; and slaves remained slaves afterwards, precisely as serfs remained serfs after Magna Charta, and peasants, peasants after the Bill of Rights, with no change whatever, but yet with every claim to be *cared for* by each body politic, as kindness and justice might from time to time require.

If this view be thought inconsistent with the broad language of the Declaration of Independence, with the equal rights into which all men "are born," it needs only to consider the specifications of the Document itself, which are found, not to be the common rights of men, as men, but the rights of Englishmen as Englishmen — rights brought by the colonists from England, and existing by charter and custom, from the first. If the specifications are not as broad as the general expression, they necessarily limit and explain

b

it; can in no way be extended by it to other people, and to other matters, than those which are specified. If there be a literal inconsistency, it cannot be helped, and must find its practical commendation and its just issue, not in admitting free Indians and enslaved Africans to the privileges of Englishmen, which would be no privileges to them, but in such use of the governing power as shall best promote the well-being of both. And in regard to it we may adopt the language of Macaulay concerning the resolution of Parliament which preceded and secured the Bill of Rights. "In fact, the one beauty of it was its inconsistency." Like that resolution, the Declaration stated and secured its great object, if not in perfect logical agreement with its general expression, yet in perfect consistency with any just view of its broadest terms. "Life, liberty, and the pursuit of happiness," to which all men are declared entitled, cannot be so understood as to interfere with either of the three. "Liberty" has "life" and "the pursuit of happiness" as its manifest and necessary limitations. The question remains with regard to all men that "are born," of all ages, sexes, classes, and conditions — *how much* liberty, in their actual case, does best promote and secure these primary and highest purposes. To be in any worthy sense equally free, that is, with reference to "life" and "the pursuit of happiness," the various classes and conditions of men must be *unequally free,* strange as the paradox may seem. In this sense, men and women, parents and children, masters and apprentices, in our own European population, *are* equally free. Who shall say that with slavery ameliorated — its bonds to labor and maintain labor retained, and its bad bonds removed — that Southern masters and their African slaves may not be equally free, that is, equally entitled to "life" and "the pursuit of happiness." When the government shall become truly patriarchal, at once in just regulation and in paternal protection, it will prove the most perfect freedom.*

3. A third mistake of our Foreign Advisers consists in demanding for slavery, as an existing fact, the same refusal as for the proposal to enslave.

No mistake is more plain. Every where and always, we must refuse the proposal to change the condition of our fellow-men from the better to the worse; but this does not require, for it does not enable us to change instantly and absolutely the worse for the better, to annihilate any or all distinctions on a scale of endless variety. Poverty, sickness, wounds, are in this respect in the same category as slavery. We may accept no proposal to inflict them, but this does not require, for it does not enable us to abolish them. All that is required, in either case, is to meet the actual condition with all kindness and justice, to alleviate all evils, and bestow all benefits, to our utmost power. We must refuse utterly and instantly the proposal to engage in highway robbery; but we are not therefore required to restore utterly and instantly the "man wounded and half dead" to soundness and his goods, but only to dress his wounds, provide for his wants, and aid his recovery according to our

---

* Compare pp. 133, 134.

power. The divine illustration of love to our neighbor requires no more.

The impossibility of treating facts, like the proposal to introduce them, lies, in the very nature of things, in the arrangements of the world — embracing toils, exposures, sufferings, of exceeding inequality from the very heights of wealth down to the deepest extremes of poverty and woe. In sober truth, it is not man but God, it is not human will but the ordinance of Heaven, which makes it the necessity of every country, and of every age, that existing conditions should be incapable of instant and absolute abolition — should admit only of alleviation and improvement. The necessity is for substance the same in Europe and America. *The labor must be done* at once for the livelihood of the laborers themselves — their employers and mankind, or all must suffer a severer doom than labor and exposure in any form which has ever been endured. The mightiest governments of earth have their limits; are not competent to remove social evils, nay, even social abuses, at their will; are restrained to the one work within their power, of gradual amelioration — none the less where the mass of the people are nominally free, none the more where they are enslaved. We proceed to name European instances, neither for reproach nor self-justification, but to make plain the principles which must govern Europe and America alike in dealing with great social facts, with existing conditions of society.

Take first the *mining* of Europe, with all its exposures and miseries — the work on which all other work depends, the labor by which all other labor is alleviated and aided, at once the severest and the most indispensable of the occupations of mankind; without which there can be no provision for multitudes of men, no ease and comfort of civilized life. *Mining* is an existing fact, an actual institution, dooming a few, compared with the whole race benefited by it, and yet thousands, to the severest labors, exposures, and sufferings, and incidentally but actually, to abuses which call for relief. And yet, it cannot be instantly and absolutely abolished, without greater evils even to the miners themselves, without damage to the whole well-being of the race, without dooming the world to a ruin worse than all the toils, exposures, sufferings, and even abuses of the mines. You cannot abolish the miner's lot, unless you can abolish God's ordinance when he built the earth and hid in its depths the treasures of iron and coal, and silver and gold, for the use of countless millions of men, — to ennoble and alleviate their labors, — to limit and lessen their exposures and sufferings, to provide more abundantly for their wants. You can no more abolish mining and the miner's lot, than you can level the mountains and raise the depths in which the stores of ages have been gathered by the hand of the Almighty — than you can command to the surface the whole material for the instruments with which the earth is tilled, and its productions wrought for the food, and raiment, and comfort of mankind, and for the very coin by which what is thus provided is distributed to the families of all nations. All you can do is to ameliorate the indispensable lot — to

b *

remove as far and as fast as possible its manifest
abuses — to make it as easy, as safe, as advantageous
to the actual miners as the indispensable labor per-
mits — leaving only the toil, exposure, and suffering
essential to the lot which God's wise providence has
ordered. The steam engine, and the safety lamp,
and the attempts of the British Parliament to correct
abuses which fill the mind with horror, all indicate
the amelioration which is possible, and not the abolition which is impossible. The miners must still be
left to their lot, in the assurance that nothing which
Heaven has arranged is without its mercy and its
lesson, without the axiom made plain to every mind
of man and taught in every lot — to prosperity in its
greatest heights, to poverty in its lowest depths, to
the miners even, in the bowels of the earth. "Surely,"
says the most ancient of all books, "there is a vein
for the silver, and a place for gold, where they fine
it. Iron is taken out of the earth, and brass is mol-
ten out of the stone. . . . There is a path which no
fowl knoweth, and which the vulture's eye hath not
seen. He putteth forth his hand upon the rock; he
overturneth the mountains by the roots. He cutteth
out rivers among the rocks, and his eye seeth every
precious thing; he bindeth the floods from overflowing; and the thing that is hid bringeth he forth to light.
But where shall wisdom be found? and where is the
place of understanding? . . . And unto man he said,
Behold the fear of the Lord, that is wisdom; and
to depart from evil is understanding."* When

* Job xxviii.

God made it needful that the replenished earth should live by mining, he did not bury the miners beneath his highest mercy, the best boon of life; beneath the reach of all the beatitudes.

The same necessity — the same paradox of toil, exposure, and suffering in order to the greatest ease, safety, and enjoyment — the same irreversible doom of some, at once for their own benefit and the benefit of all — the same liability to abuse, and the same moral opportunity, — belong to the great mass of mankind, occupied in the labors by which men live, and for which mining provides the indispensable material; — the same impossibility of immediate and absolute abolition, and even of the abuses at any time actual, but not essential to the doom. There can be no immediate and absolute abolition of the condition of the laboring classes of Europe — of " the poor," the " lower classes," the " peasantry," the " operatives " — at the best, dependent on scanty wages, and at the worst, " suffering masses " outnumbering the means of employment and support. This condition of the laborers of Europe is an existing fact, to be met in all kindness and justice by individuals and governments, as a fact to be regarded, — but not as a proposal to be instantly and absolutely rejected. Parliaments, Kings, Emperors cannot turn great national facts into non-existence — cannot put them into mere proposals — can no more emancipate " the poor," the " lower classes," the " peasantry," the " operatives," the " serfs," of their several governments, than they can emancipate the miners from their lot, — than they can emancipate the human race from the use of iron, and coal, and silver, and gold, and food, and raiment, and house, and home. All they can do, is by all the means in their power to alleviate the miseries and correct the abuses of every lot.

Suppose it assumed on our side the Atlantic, that the system of small farming and a working yeomanry in our Northern States, is the true idea of social well-being, and that we require all Europe to adopt it — instantly and absolutely to emancipate "the poor," to raise to social equality "the lower classes," to abolish the poverty of "the masses," to divide the wide domains of unenlightened ages, and establish every where laborers on their little farms after the manner of New England.

Vain and absurd demand! as impossible as to remove the mountains! If it were a proposal to bring the New England yeomanry into the condition of the European "poor," there would be reason and conscience in rejecting it. If Europe had the power, it would have no right to force upon us the undesirable change, to rob us of our birthright enjoyment — of the gift of Providence inherited from our fathers. But it is quite another thing to undertake the impossibility of putting *their* masses into our condition — of changing the doom which Providence has imposed as the inheritance from many generations. What God has permitted to grow for ages, man has no power to change in a day. He may reject the proposal to plant the seed, but he cannot uproot the stern growth of centuries.

Vain and absurd demand! The very pattern we propose for Europe to follow, only illustrates the im-

possibility of following it. How came that condition
of the laboring masses in America which is proposed
as a pattern to the greater masses of Europe ? Came
it at the instant, at the call of man or by the decree
of any government on earth, that you should require
Sovereigns and Parliaments to " charm " it into being ?
Rather, did it not require a new world for the theatre
of a minute experiment, and the slow emigration of
a medium class, " the siftings of three kingdoms," and
then the time of two centuries, to establish governments, create habits, and form communities capable
of assimilating and absorbing *moderate* proportions of
the European peasantry ? The governments of New
England, New York, Pennsylvania, the models of the
North, could not have been instituted *at all*, by the
crowds of European peasants now thronging our
shores. If their emigration had been rapid at first,
the New England condition of a working yeomanry
would never have existed on our continent, nor been
capable of its present work of assimilation and ab-
sorption. Even now, there are complaints that they
come too fast, whether for their advantage or our
own. What else means our " Americanism," our ob-
jection to the ingress of these hundreds of thousands
every year, but our dread of a too rapid increase of
the European " lower classes ; " — but our acknowledg-
ment, that a population homogeneous with ourselves
cannot come instantly into the full inheritance of the
lot which the providence of two hundred years has
given us; that Europe cannot change by decree the
condition of the masses of her people ; must leave
them to their inherited doom, with only those allevi-

ations and benefits which kindness and justness can bestow — those progressive improvements of which they can only plant the seed and cherish the growth.

The impossibility of annihilating great social facts, as the proposal to introduce them might be rejected, applies equally to the most despotic and to the most republican of the European Powers. The Russian Autocrat and the British Parliament are alike impotent to change the existing conditions of the masses of their people. The nobility and the serfs of the one, the aristocracy and peasantry, with the middle classes, of the other, exist in fixed relations of poverty and wealth, neither at the bidding nor the forbidding of "the powers that be." The Parliament, were it ever so much inclined to benefit the whole people — to bless the masses — the Autocrat, with whatever wisdom and good will — have their necessary limit — are precluded by the circumstances actually existing, by the rooted strength of ages, from instant and absolute change. There is no power in governments, despotic or free, to enrich "the poor," to raise "the lower classes," to banish the "misery of the masses," to emancipate "the serfs," to change the condition of European laborers into that of the working yeomanry of New England, as there is to reject any proposal to bring the working yeomanry of these States into the condition of European serfs and peasants. All that can be done, and all that is required, is, according to the abilities of the several governments, and the capabilities of the several people, to bestow such reliefs and benefits as are possible in the conditions actually existing — such as are continually attempted

by the British Parliament for England, Scotland, and
Wales, and even for Ireland itself, only with a wisdom
and kindness never to pause until the utmost limits
of well-being have been reached. The Russian Autocrat can do no more — will find himself hindered or
baffled in his endeavors, if in his desire for rapid improvement, he transcends the bounds which conditions,
established by ages, have made as firm as the mountains. These bounds he may or may not have suf-
ficiently regarded, in providing for the freedom of
serfs homogeneous with the higher classes of society.
Time alone can settle the question whether he have
retained duly the bonds which make free, and duly
rejected the freedom which enslaves. There are limits, on the one side and on the other, to the proposals
of the Czar. Some bonds are retained upon both masters and serfs, no doubt designed to prevent in Russia
the great evil of Southern Europe — of masses " mis-
erably free." In Russia, now, as in all the world
and in all time, then only can beneficial changes be
wrought in long established conditions of society,
when mutual relations and obligations are duly regarded, in view of the whole past conditions of the
people; then only can the well-being of its serfs be
duly provided for, when the mutual dependence of
property and labor is duly regarded, when bad bonds
are progressively broken, and good bonds retained
and strengthened. The nineteenth century, civilization, Christianity, instead of requiring, forbid the
immediate and absolute abolition of Russian serfdom — instead of forbidding, require some bonds
retained upon the existing and long established prop-

erty of the country; and if so, some bonds on the existing and long established labor of the country also, that property may be able to fulfil its obligations;—while at the same time, there is forbidden every abuse and required every possible amelioration and advantage for the whole people, whether bond or free.

The impossibility of immediate and absolute change in actual social conditions, even in homogeneous Europe, has always existed. The Europe that now calls upon America to treat the fact of African slavery like the proposal to enslave, has given proof for ages, that it asks an impossibility. In truth, the existing conditions of any period of its history, as they were never due to the governments of that period, but to previous acts and methods which gave them their prevalence, so they were out of the power of cotemporary authority, except by such corrections and ameliorations as might grow at length into beneficial substitutes. European serfdom was not the infliction of the lords of the soil, paramount at any period, but the growth of ages; partly from the original barbarian condition, partly by conquest and oppression, and partly by methods of relief and security to which various exposures gave rise. Originating with the barbarism of the European nations, the low condition of the masses might have proved worse, might have continued longer, if feudalism had not intervened with its protecting, governing, and providing care, as well as its oppression.* The barbarian starting-points, and the element

* Guizot, vol. iii. pp. 122, 123.

of conquest and subjugation, are older than Julius
Cæsar who describes them; — even Great Britain
having been visited by continental conquerors and
settlers, before the Roman, the Saxon, the Danish,
and the Norman invasions, by which its enserfed condition became extended and established — at every
point, beyond the removal of any cotemporary governments.

The impossibility thus due to long established
social conditions and belonging to European serfdom,
explains the chasm of history in regard to its abolition. *There is no history, because there could be none.* No
direct, positive, absolute and general emancipation
was ever made by any decree or succession of de-
crees of which history could make record; — the emancipation, such as it was, being every where only casual
and incidental, the growth of time and circumstance,
the only method possible of changing the condition
of the masses of the people in all countries and
all times.

Indeed, whatever condemnation may be due to
those warlike tribes, the Franks, the Saxons and the
Normans, who conquered and enserfed the European
masses, when each new step of serfdom was a proposal capable of being refused; — whether a condition
advancing by conquest and oppression be regarded
as an unmixed evil, or as a providential method of
evolving modern industry and civilization from the
indolence and improvidence of savage life; — *after
the deed was done,* and established relations and conditions existed, there was no power in European
monarchs or lords to abolish the actual institution —

c

to do more than to correct and ameliorate up to the just relations of property and labor. "No great fact, no social state makes its appearance complete and at once."* "The change, great as it was, (in Great Britain,) was the effect of gradual development, not of demolition and reconstruction. The exorbitant power of the Barons was gradually reduced, the condition of the peasants gradually elevated. . . . That revolution which put an end to property in man, was silently and imperceptibly effected."† "The evil was mingled with the institutions of the country, and required much time and successive efforts for its eradication."‡

The impossibility of immediate and absolute change is still more manifest in the issues of even this slow emancipation, — silently and imperceptibly effected, as alone was possible, making it a caution and not a pattern, and requiring in all future attempts some new method not included in the received idea of emancipation and freedom. There is manifest enough (on which we have dwelt§) "the misery of the masses," indicating that in the slow progress from serfdom there was not a sufficient reservation of mutual bonds; and there *were*, certainly, for many ages, extreme social difficulties and disorders, due undoubtedly, in degree, to the premature and indiscreet emancipation of lords and serfs — to "too free a freedom." The just view forced itself upon the mind of Puffendorf, more than a century ago, in view of evils

* Guizot, vol. iii. p. 17.   † Macaulay, vol. i. pp. 21, 23.
‡ A History of the Poor Law, by Sir George Nicholas, Secretary of the Poor Law Board.
§ See Chapter VI. "European Experiments with Serfdom."

of which there is history enough. "To be held within
the limits of slavery which the natural law of support
prescribes, apart from the cruelty of some masters and
the rigor of certain laws, — in this, there is no undue
severity. For this compulsory subjection is compen-
sated by the advantage of being assured of a livelihood, whilst hired laborers know not often how to
subsist, whether for want of being hired or their own
laziness, which cannot be cured without blows. This
laziness men have endeavored to remedy, by the
establishment of workhouses, a sort of prison, to make
men work, whether they will or no. Some have
thought, not without reason, that the prohibition of
slavery among Christian nations, hath chiefly occa-
sioned that flood of thieving vagrants and sturdy
beggars which is usually complained of."* The same
view forces itself upon those who are occupied at the
present day in the endeavor to remedy the conse-
quences of ancient mistakes by new legislation. Sir
George Nicholas, in his elaborate history of the poor
laws, says: "The change from a state of slavery was
attended with a certain amount of evil — led to a
great increase of vagrancy. That there was cause for
coercive legislation, cannot be denied." He accord-
ingly refers to the laws of centuries to compel labor
and to supply the wants of the poor — from Edward
II. to Elizabeth, ending in those famous poor laws,
rendered necessary by the condition of society, and
intended to be equally binding upon property and
labor, of the one-sided application of which Black-

* Puffendorf, Book VI. chap. iii. sec. 10.

stone complains.* However lacking history is in
regard to emancipation from serfdom, there is no lack
of record of the fearful condition of society which was
the consequence, when the police and provision of
serfdom ceased to be compulsory on property and
labor, and the only remedy men saw was a partial
restoration of the bonds prematurely broken. Surely
the abolition of serfdom in Europe, though slow
enough, was premature and indiscreet, and is not an
example to be followed, but a caution to be carefully
regarded; requiring, wherever slavery is found, all
just bonds retained both on property and labor, —
some indispensable coercion upon both, in order that
the functions of both may be duly performed; —
preventing the idleness and improvidence which a
premature freedom might give to the laborer, and
the parsimony and neglect which a premature freedom might give to the employer; — taking before-
hand the same liberty which in every land the most
free nations are compelled to take — in requiring
property to support the poor, and the poor to work
according to their ability.

These European instances illustrate the principles
applicable to both continents alike, and are only the
more imperative in America on account of wide differences in civilization and race. If actual conditions of
men essentially homogeneous cannot be instantly and
absolutely abolished, and when abolished by slow degrees and unobserved processes, have furnished instances of warning and caution instead of encourage-

---

* See "Slavery and the Remedy," p. 39.

ment, how doubly impossible the work, when the
ruling and the subject races have such remarkable
differences;—the African not only lower in the social
scale by direct inheritance from barbarian ancestors,
but marked by physical characteristics, which always
distinguish him. No European successes could decide
in favor of the immediate and absolute emancipation
of African slaves and American masters. How much
more is the example withdrawn, and a double impossibility assured by European *ill* success, even with
a homogeneous people and emancipation by slow
degrees. Vagabondage and violence requiring law,
and law, failing to recover from vagabondage and
violence — wide-spread pauperism requiring relief,
and all measures of relief failing to provide for that
wide-spread pauperism — centuries passed, and still
showing "miserable masses," which baffle the wisest
legislation and philanthropy, where the people are
essentially of one blood — these results of European
emancipation, all-pervading, long-enduring, and, to all
human view, irretrievable, — how distinctly and sol-
emnly do they forewarn the greater difficulty, the
more absolute impossibility in the matter of African
slavery in America, — opening to the view a "misery
of the masses" of which homogeneous Europe cannot furnish a type.*

* In requiring an ameliorated slavery, instead of instant and absolute freedom for the benefit of the African race, as lower in the social scale, we ab-
stain, as in the work itself, from any assertion of their natural inferiority, as
entirely irrelevant to the question; — assured that the rights of one race over
another have not been submitted to their own judgment of superiority; that
no claim to be "the Celestial Empire" can give Heaven's authority, either to
enslave or hold in slavery any portion of mankind. We simply take the facts

c *

The difficulties belonging to differences of civilization and race are abundantly set forth in the original work,* and in the subsequent Review of the Decision of the Supreme Court in the case of Dred Scott. There are intrinsic difficulties — there may be also unreasonable prejudice; but both unite in the argument *against* immediate and absolute emancipation, for something better than immediate and absolute freedom. "The laws which have been passed and enforced by the States most exposed to large proportions of free African population, and the reasons given for those laws, show most plainly, that there is not 'free soil' for the freed African in all our wide America. With the minutest exceptions, in every town, and county, and state, North as well as South, every body thinks that the African race, improved though they have been, since their emigration, are not entitled to be, in large numbers, part and parcel with the Anglo-Saxon race — to be advantageously to themselves or the whole people, parts of the several 'Englands' of the new world."

as they are, without deciding how they might have been, if the circumstances of the two races had been interchanged, or how they may become hereafter. It is enough for our argument, that the African *is* less advanced in civilization and its adjuncts, even though admitted equally capable of advancement, and his actual inferiority were referred entirely to the providential arrangement, which fixed his place of habitation on the earth. Dare the European race proudly say, that if God had assigned *them* their place behind the great African Desert and in the depths of the torrid zone, and had given temperate Europe to the Negro, with its gulfs, and bays, and rivers, for the easy communication of civilization and Christianity from their great centres, that the Negro of the nineteenth century would not have been the superior, in all that can exalt and bless mankind? Whatever might or might not have been, — the barbarism of Central Africa is an actual fact, has been only partially removed from the race in the United States, and must be taken into the account in any proposals for their well-being.

* Pages 21, 80, and 129—132.

If any thing be wanted to intensify the argument from the differences of civilization and race, it may be had in the words of the great champion* of free soil, in his speech on Kansas, in the Senate of the United States, March 3, 1858. "Free labor," says the Senator, "has at last apprehended its rights, its interests, its powers, its destiny, and is organizing itself to assume the government of the Republic. It will meet you every where, in the Territories and out of them, wherever you may go to extend slavery. It has driven you back in California and Kansas. It will invade you soon in Delaware, Maryland, Virginia, Missouri, and Texas. It will meet you in Arizona, in Central America, and even in Cuba. You may, indeed, get a start under or near the Tropics, but it will be for a short time. Even there, you will found states for free labor to maintain and occupy." . . . "The interests of the white race demand the ultimate emancipation of all ,men. The white man needs this continent to labor on. His head is clear, his arm is strong, and his necessities are fixed. *He must and will have it.*" Alas, how extremes meet! The highest philanthropy and the deepest cruelty are at one! The demand is for freedom for the African race, and yet they are not to have room for the sole of their foot!—there is to be no "free soil for the freed African in all our wide America"! Surely, there is an overruling Providence which turns men's counsels against themselves, and makes them to establish what they intended to destroy. There is no argument so

---

* Hon. W. H. Seward.

intense against immediate and absolute abolition, and in favor of an ameliorated and protecting slavery, as is furnished by the expressions and practices of the advocates of free soil in the United States.

The conclusion from European instances — more decisive in view of differences of race — is required by the whole history of mankind; an immediate and absolute abolition of a great social institution has never occurred since the world began : — rather, *never but once*, and then, under such conditions as make the impossibility only the more plain, when it is proposed as the mere work of man under the common providence of God : *once, and once only ;* — the exception proving the rule, by which the most powerful nations must needs govern themselves in their undertakings for the masses of their people. It was only by the strong hand and outstretched arm of the Almighty, over-ruling the universal laws which govern human things, that the threefold impossibility was accomplished in favor of the tribes of Israel instantly and absolutely released from Egyptian bondage. *Miracles* from heaven delivered them from the power which held them in slavery — *miracles* opened their path through the sea, and fed, and clothed, and governed, and taught, and disciplined them, forty years in the wilderness, until a new generation was prepared for settlement in the promised land : and *miracles* prepared for them their final habitation, giving them houses which they builded not, wells which they digged not, and fields which they planted not : — the whole, most manifestly, withdrawing their example, unless the same commands, the same signs and wonders require again what is utterly impossible, and therefore not required, under the common providence of God. The whole history of mankind, with this single exception, itself joining the testimony, confirms our conclusion from general principles and European experiments, that immediate and absolute emancipation is impossible, and must be doubly impossible in the case of African slavery in the United States.

———————

This confident assurance has not been adopted without considering the example of the British West Indies, concerning which claims so opposite are urged. Instead of attempting to decide upon conflicting testimony, we have preferred to admit in degree the most favorable accounts, and to maintain the alleged impossibility notwithstanding. Admitting, then, all that is claimed by the most sanguine friends of emancipation in the West Indies, we assert that its success is neither so assured nor so complete as to make it an example for the United States if the cases were alike; while they are plainly so unlike, that the restricted and regulated emancipation in the one, if the success were assured and complete, would require restrictions and regulations in the other suited to the case, and in our belief, the ameliorated slavery which this work proposes.

1. The success of West India emancipation is neither so assured nor so complete as to make it an example. It is plainly too early in its history

to give assurance of success. The Bishop of Barbadoes, expecting final success, admits that there are many evils, but claims that two or even three generations are needful, before the ill effects of slavery can be entirely removed, and the success of emancipation be complete.[*] Be it so. But then, also, it is equally right to say, that two or three generations must pass before the *good* effects of slavery can be lost, and the *ill* success of the emancipation be complete. In truth, a longer time is required before either the good or the evil issues can be decided by experience. Though there were at the end of twenty years no occasion for misgiving in regard to those whose habits of life, and relations to property and skill, were so suddenly changed, a longer trial would be needful to determine the question. Much more, when there are acknowledged evils as well as hopeful appearances, it must be impossible to decide whether the one or the other be due to the slavery abolished or to the freedom bestowed. If the evils remaining may be referred to the influences of slavery, which it requires two or three generations to remove, then may any hopeful appearances be referred to the influences of slavery not yet entirely vanished away. The old habits of labor on the one hand, and of capital and arrangement on the other, may not yet have lost their force, and there may be remaining some of the advantages of a regular and regulated industry — of due labor and maintenance, preventing the evils of " too free a freedom," but giving no assurance

---

[*] Letter dated Feb. 23, 1858, in National Era, Aug. 12.

of a favorable issue when that force is lost. The "train" does not instantly stop when the "power" is removed, but goes forward almost as before. Nevertheless, gravitation and friction are producing their gradual effect, and the whole force will be expended at last. Admit all the favorable appearances claimed, and they give no absolute assurance of a successful emancipation.

Besides the uncertainty of the final issues, the success at its present stage is manifestly too incomplete to make a decisive example. Difficulties and evils are admitted which break the charm, and throw us back upon general principles and the whole experience of mankind. Such admissions as those of the Bishop of Barbadoes and others, with regard to Barbadoes and the smaller islands where the circumstances are peculiarly favorable, give ground for the assertion that even in them the success is too incomplete to become our example. Much more do the larger islands, as we understand the admissions of the friends of emancipation, give this ground, in greater degrees of idleness, improvidence, and vagrancy, forewarning the evils which prevailed in Europe for centuries, and have issued in the "miserable masses" of the nineteenth century, with whatever enhancement differences of race and climate may produce.

That the success of West India emancipation is thus incomplete, is confirmed by certain important facts which admit of no other explanation. How else can we explain the act of the Legislature of Jamaica, meeting idleness and vagrancy with such provisions as to be objected to by Lord Brougham, in the House of Lords, as "reducing the free negro population to slavery."* Laws are provided for occasions, which, however exaggerated, can never be entirely non-existent. There must be idleness and vagrancy, with the fear of their increase, or such a law could never have been proposed.

The actual evils and the dreaded danger are implied, also, in the methods of emancipation proposed by other European governments having tropical possessions, viz., the retaining some good bonds, instead of loosing all, in order that the evils and dangers of the British West Indies may be avoided. Thus, the Dutch ordinance for liberating fifty thousand slaves in Surinam, *retains bonds*, instead of making emancipation complete. Says the Kingston Journal, "Upon being liberated, the slaves are not to be left unconditionally to their own control, and the control of those who are ready to take advantage of their ignorance to impose upon them, as in this and the other British colonies. At the same time, the former slave-holders are protected against the evils arising from the want of labor, as the emancipated will not become the unrestricted owners of their own time and labor. The duties they are to perform are to be made known by general orders, but all slaves who shall repay to the government the amount paid for their freedom, are to be exempt from these orders. Another, and by far one of the most wholesome provisions in the law, is that all who obtain their freedom are to contribute on fixed terms towards a fund for

* London Morning Chronicle, March 23, 1858.

repaying the government the cost of their freedom — also for religious teaching, education of children, nursing of the sick and relief of the poor and aged. With us in the West Indies, the absence of such regulations at the general emancipation, involved us in difficulties, against which at the present time we have to fight a hard battle."

The Danish method at Santa Cruz indicates a like caution — requiring, as we understand, an " annual affiliation " — the only freedom being the power of changing masters and service, without the liberty to have no master, or to strike for higher wages.

It does not answer the argument to ascribe the evils acknowledged to the proprietors and not to the laborers — to the emancipated masters and not to the emancipated slaves. It only gives prominence to the necessity of bonds upon property, that labor may have due opportunity and provision, while it requires, of course, corresponding bonds on labor, without which bonds on property would be of no avail. If the emancipated masters have used their freedom unjustly towards the native-born laborers, *they* were made too free, and should have remained under some of their former bonds. But then, of necessity, the slaves also were made too free, and should have remained under such bonds as would enable the masters to fulfil their obligations.

Neither does it answer the argument to produce instances of African advancement in property and station ; for the all-important question is, the effect upon the mass, and not upon excepted cases. Besides, a just amelioration could not fail to secure *more*

d

excepted cases without the evils resulting from the whole system of labor and provision abolished. The "misery of the masses" in England is not less deplorable, because out of "the poor," "the peasantry," "the operatives," individuals sometimes rise to wealth and rank. In this case also, wiser measures for the masses would no doubt have resulted in more instances of individual advancement, without the evil of wide-spread wretchedness.

2. But the two cases are plainly *unlike*, — emancipation in the West Indies, being with bonds remaining and imposed, impossible in the United States, and requiring some corresponding bonds suited to our different condition. Let the actual bonds of the emancipated colonies be briefly stated and duly compared.

There is then, first, the physical condition and relations. The insular position itself, and in the islands where the success is most confidently affirmed, the narrow limits, render labor still dependent upon property, and property still dependent upon labor, as before emancipation, — are bonds upon both, impossible in our continental position. The climate also — within the Tropics — protects African labor from European competition, obliges the property in the soil to employ the laborers born upon the soil, and protects them from the "clear head and strong arm and fixed necessities" and determined will of the white man: again, an impossible bond even at our remotest South — and more and more impossible as we approach the North.

There is, next, the political condition of the emancipated colonies : — the British government — direct, positive, powerful, prompt, in its colonial administration — with its actual and visible array, inspiring a sense of unavailing resistance and impossible escape — the "arcanum of empire" — always ready to exert its reserved power — acting when it does not act — vigorous when inert — governing when it does not govern, by its prestige of promptness and efficiency.

And this prompt and efficient government has no need to await the consent of the governed mass, unqualified and new to the work of self-government — to await the making or the executing of the laws by which they may be directed or restrained, as must be the case with us if the freed slaves are admitted to equal privileges with the white race, — to our universal suffrage. The property or rental which makes a voter in the British West Indies excludes the mass of freed negroes, and leaves them therefore under the bonds of law and police which the property of the country — the minority of the whole people — may see fit to retain or renew, subject only to that royal authority and power which gives efficiency to their own. Surely there are needful with us some corresponding bonds suited to the fact of universal suffrage.

Moreover, this prompt and efficient government, unhindered in its action, has more than its own inherent potency and prestige — it has actual direction and restraint, *special regulations and provisions*, new bonds in place of old bonds loosed, to be enforced if need be, with its whole array of power, and therefore

not likely to need enforcement. Thus, in Antigua, says
the Superintendent of Police, "The numerical force
of this district is eleven sergeants and two officers.
Five of these sergeants are on duty every twenty-
four hours. One remains in charge of the premises,
arms, and stores. Four patrol night and day, and
have also to attend to the duties of the magistrate, and
the other is employed by me in general patrol duties,
pointing out nuisances and irregularities. . . . . A
due fear of, and prompt obedience to, the authority of
the magistrates, is a prominent feature of the lower
orders, and to this ['bond'] I attribute, mainly, the
maintenance of rural tranquillity." * At Barbadoes,
also, where emancipation is considered specially successful, there *is*, as reported by a resident there the
very last winter, (1858,) "a large and most efficient
Police, armed with clubs, and recognized by appro-
priate badges, with a signal post, by means of which
the whole police force can be concentrated on any
point, and if needful, sustained by the whole military
force of the island. Surely the conclusion is just —
insular position — climate — efficient and prompt
government, and special regulations and provisions —
are bonds — and if the 'quasi' emancipation were
ever so successful, the example would require in our
wide-spread continent, temperate climate, universal
suffrage, and inefficient Police, some corresponding
bonds — some 'quasi' slavery."

These are some of the reasons for our confident
assurance from general principles and the whole
course of history, that the absolute and immediate abo-

* Thome & Kimball, pp. 44, 45.

lition of slavery in the United States is impossible — the example of the British West Indies notwithstanding — that whatever refusal may be required on any proposal to enslave anew, nothing can now be done but with Christian kindness and wisdom, to retain those bonds upon property and labor, which are manifestly for the well-being of the whole people, of the African as well as the European race. The facts of slavery are as real and as stubborn as the mountains, and are not to be brushed away as if they were feathers. We can no more place the three millions of African slaves in the condition of the Northern yeomanry, or of the free whites at large, than we can replace them in the savage wilds from which their ancestors were torn; or, than we can do for them in one year what Providence has done with ourselves in two thousand of European and not African opportunity, and two hundred of cis-Atlantic discipline. The question is not now whether we shall steal men from Africa, and bring them through all the horrors of the middle passage *into* slavery, but how shall we meet the actual case of millions of slaves existing and increasing in our land.

To this question there is but one just answer: At whatever inconvenience the dominant race, individually and socially, must provide for the real well-being of the millions committed to its charge, according to its individual and social power, with equal good-will to the African as the European race — none the less to the African because he is enslaved; none the more to the European because he is free.*

* Chapters IV. — VI.

d *

To this end of well-being is this work devoted. Allowing the proper essence of slavery, viz., the *being held to labor*, with the corresponding obligation to *maintain labor*, it requires that an existing institution, by which millions eat their bread and the wants of the race are provided for, shall not be abolished but retained; while all the ills which are not of its essence shall be carefully and wisely mitigated or removed, and all advantages added which are possible in the actual case.

It is in aid of this high purpose, and not for base and wicked ends, that we have invoked a NEW ERA* in Northern as well as Southern opinion and effort, instead of the vain and useless struggle to limit and abolish on the one hand, or to perpetuate and extend on the other; — a calm, deliberate, and persevering attempt to introduce "counsels and methods as acceptable to the South as to the North, and as advantageous to the African as the European race in their mysterious relations to each other."

It is with the same high purpose that we turn now from our own country to Europe, and invoke a NEW ERA in the opinions and counsels of our Foreign advisers: — not for evil, but for good — not for wrong, but for right; not for the oppression and ruin of the African race, but for their protection and advancement. We implore them not to encourage the vain struggle of equibalanced sections by appeals to the whole United States in a matter for which each separate State is alone responsible — not to require of America a political consistency of which Europe furnishes

---

* Page 120.

no example, and which is forbidden by the condition of the people to whom they claim its application;— and lastly, not to demand of the United States of America, with its incongenial races, an immediate and absolute change, which Europe never made with its peoples of one blood, and in the work of ages, failed of advantageous results; and that, instead, they will aid us in the only proper work for Christian philanthropists, joining that fellowship of impotence* to which we have called our Northern countrymen, as their mightiest power for African WELL-BEING:

* Page 74.